Red Robin Books is an imprint of Corner To Learn Limited

Published by
Corner To Learn Limited
Willow Cottage • 26 Purton Stoke
Swindon • Wiltshire SN5 4JF • UK

ISBN 978-0-9545353-6-0

Text © Neil Griffiths and Scott Mann 2001
Illustrations © Judith Blake 2001
First published in the UK 2001
Reprinted 2003, 2005, 2007

Design by
David Rose

Printed by
Tien Wah Press Pte. Ltd., Singapore

The Journey

In memory of Scott - a free spirit

by Neil Griffiths and Scott Mann

Illustrated by Judith Blake

On a windy autumn day,
A boat b-r-o-k-e free and sailed away.

Swiftly floating out of sight ....

It bobbed and weaved into the night.

Underneath the star-filled sky,
Our little boat passed mountains high.

As the dawn began to break,

The stream became a peaceful lake.

Battered, bashed, bumped and tossed,
Our little boat was nearly lost.

Reaching waters far below,

The sailing boat began to s l o w.

Floating past a church and farm,
It drifted on through waters calm.

Next it reached a busy town,
Where rubbish turned the water brown.

Here amongst the slime and muck,
Our little boat got truly STUCK!

Not until a springtime flood,
Did it escape the sticky mud.

Heading down the estuary,

It glided gently out to sea.........

Here amongst the weeds it lay,

Until a boy came by one day ...

Neil Griffiths is a former Primary School headteacher and the creator of the internationally-acclaimed and award-winning Storysack® concept. He has a passion for children's literature and his many books feature strong storylines, memorable characters, enchanting language, and arresting illustrations.

Neil loves to tell a story and storytime with him is a rare and highly entertaining event as he magically draws his audience into his storyworlds. For more information on Neil's storytime sessions, inspirational training workshops or his many other books, visit his website at: **www.redrobinbooks.com**.

Other books by **Neil Griffiths**

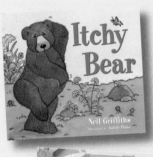

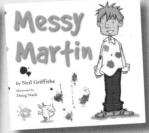

Red Robin
BOOKS
Where story matters

www.redrobinbooks.com